WUPH
THEATER

Martha on the Case

Adaptation by Jamie White
Based on a TV series teleplay written by Matt Steinglass
Based on the characters created by Susan Meddaugh

HOUGHTON MIFFLIN HARCOURT
Boston • New York • 2010

Daniel
Helen's dad
Mariela
Helen's mom
Helen
Martha's
best friend
Jake
Helen's baby
brother
Carolina
Helen's fashionable
older cousin
Martha
the talking dog
33

Truman
Helen's smart and
curious friend
T.D.
Helen's good
and loyal friend
Alice
Helen's athletic
but clumsy friend
Skits
the family's
non-talking dog

Library of Congress Cataloging-in-Publication Data is on file.

Design by Stephanie Cooper and Bill Smith Studio

ISBN: 978-0-547-36894-8

www.hmhbooks.com
www.marthathetalkingdog.com

Manufactured in China
LEO 10 9 8 7 6 5 4 3 2 1

MARTHA SAYS HELLO

Get ready for . . . action! Danger! Doggy biscuits!

In other words, get ready for this book starring me, Martha the talking dog!

Ever since my owner Helen fed me her alphabet soup, I've been able to speak. And speak and speak . . . No one's sure how or why,

but the letters in the soup traveled up to my brain instead of down to my stomach.

Now, as long as I eat my daily bowl of alphabet soup, I can talk. To my family—Helen, baby Jake, Mom, Dad, and our non-talking dog, Skits. To Helen's best human friend, T.D. To anyone who'll listen, really.

Sometimes my family wishes I didn't talk *quite* so much. But who can argue with a talking dog? Besides, my speaking comes in handy. One night I witnessed a burglar break in to our house. No kidding. I saw him with my own eyes. I called 911 and saved the day!

Of course, I can speak to other dogs—and cats, too. But cats can be trouble. Take the time I went to Alice Boxwood's party. I made the mistake of talking to her cat, Nelson. And, well, read on to see what happened . . .

Part One
AN INVITATION

It was an ordinary day in Wagstaff City.

Helen and T.D. had eaten lunch outside the yogurt shop. Martha sat in her usual place by their feet, ready to catch any little bite that came her way.

"Yum!" said Martha, still tasting that last piece of burger. "Like I always say, the best seat in the house is under the table."

They were almost ready to go when something happened.

While Helen wasn't looking, T.D. swiped at her plate.

Helen raised her head. She looked at her food. "Okay, where did it go?"

"Where did what go?" T.D. said. "I'm innocent! I didn't do it!"

"Yes, you did," said Helen. "You're guilty."

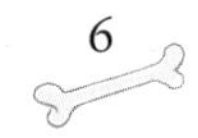

"No, I'm not. Where's your evidence?"

"Look at my plate," Helen said. "I had one fry. Now I have none. Plus, you have french fry stuck between your teeth."

"Rats!" T.D. said, covering his mouth. "Where?"

Helen smiled. "Actually, I made that up."

"You win!" T.D. said. "I did it. Guilty as charged."

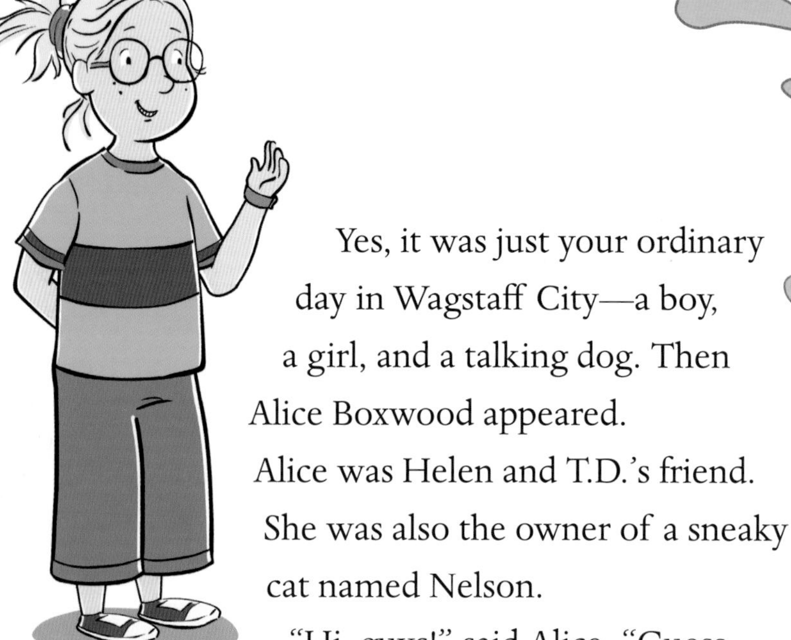

Yes, it was just your ordinary day in Wagstaff City—a boy, a girl, and a talking dog. Then Alice Boxwood appeared.

Alice was Helen and T.D.'s friend. She was also the owner of a sneaky cat named Nelson.

"Hi, guys!" said Alice. "Guess what? You're all invited!"

"To what?" T.D. asked.

"My birthday party!" Alice said, holding up invitations for the three of them.

"NOOOO!" Helen shouted.

"AHHHH!" T.D. screamed at the same time.

"Hooray!" Martha said. "My first party!"

Martha was so excited that she'd forgotten what Helen had told her about Alice's parties. They always ended with a bang. Or a crash! Or a *kaboom!*

When Alice turned three, she tried to blow out her candles. But she leaned in too far. *SPLAT!* The kids got their cake in a surprising way when Alice fell face-first into it.

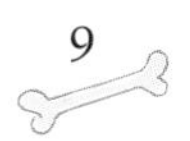

Two years ago, Alice had a make-your-own-sundae party. But the only thing Alice made was a mess. She tripped into a tray of sundaes. Ice cream splattered everywhere. (This was later known as Alice's *wear*-your-own-sundae party.)

Then last year was the year of miniature golf. Alice had a great swing, but her aim was not very good. Her balls flew in every direction except the hole. One golf ball hit the windmill on the next tee and jammed the gears of a water wheel. The wheel broke away.

"Run for your lives!" T.D. had shouted.

Alice Boxwood's parties were not for the faint of heart.

"Don't worry," said Alice. "This year I'm having a costume party. Come dressed as your favorite invention."

"My favorite invention?" said Martha. "I'm a huge fan of the sausage. Whoever invented it is a genius! Then there's the chew toy, the comfy chair, and—"

"Great. See you there!" said Alice, walking away.

Helen looked worried. "We'd better dress as bubble wrap," she said.

"Or a suit of armor," T.D. grumbled.

NELSON'S QUESTION

On the day of Alice's party, Helen was still a little nervous. But Martha couldn't wait. Her tail wagged in excited circles as she followed Helen down the street.

"I love my costume," Martha said. "The doggy door! It's the greatest invention since meat!"

"Here we are," Helen said, stopping in front of a house.

Martha's tail stopped wagging.

"Oh, no!" Martha said. "The party is at Alice's *house?*"

"What's wrong?" Helen asked.

Martha was looking at a large, fluffy cat with beady yellow eyes sitting on Alice's front porch.

"Nelson," said Martha with a shudder. "That cat is trouble."

"Come on," said Helen. "The party is in the backyard. You'll have fun. Besides, how much trouble could one little kitty cat be?"

"You don't know Nelson," Martha said. But she followed Helen to the backyard.

The yard was decorated with hot air balloons and other aircraft. The guests were dressed as all kinds of inventions. Alice greeted them in a parachute costume.

"What do you think?" Alice said. "My parents really got into the whole invention thing."

"I'll say," said Martha, looking around. "Helen, is that lipstick over there your cousin Carolina?"

"Yes," said Helen.

Then something on the other side of the yard caught Martha's attention.

"Wow! That's the biggest hot dog I've ever seen," she said. "This is my kind of party!"

"Martha!" Helen said. "That's not a real hot dog. That's T.D."

"He's with the robot clown my parents hired," Alice said, wincing.

HD
HD

RX

Alice walked to the middle of the yard where everyone could see her.

"Attention, everyone!" she announced. "It's game time! Who wants to play pin-the-tail-on-the-donkey?"

She raised a sharp pin into the air.

"AAAAH!" everyone screamed. Who knew what Alice might do with a sharp object?

"I have a better game," Martha said quickly. "It's called give-the-dog-a-biscuit."

"Phew," said Helen. "Great idea, Martha. How do you play?"

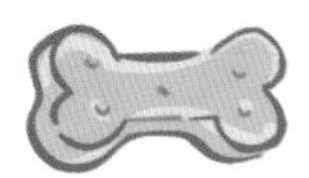

Martha told Alice to find a box of doggy biscuits. Then she explained how to play.

"Truman, you go first," said Alice. "You're the brain of the group."

Helen's neighbor Truman stepped forward. Alice handed him a biscuit and blindfolded him.

"I can't see a thing," Truman said as Alice stepped away.

"Perfect," said Martha. In a flash, she snatched the biscuit from Truman's hand and gobbled it up.

"A winner!" she cried.

"But I didn't even start yet," Truman said.

"Then let's try again," Martha said. "Another biscuit, please?"

But as soon as Truman had the biscuit in his hand, Martha snatched it and ate it.

Martha ate biscuit after biscuit until all of the biscuits were gone. And still, no one had figured out how the game worked.

"But who won?" T.D. asked.

"You're *all* winners!" Martha said. "*BURP!* Thanks for letting me play."

Martha left the puzzled guests and waddled to a quiet corner of the yard. She found a big stick and began to play with it.

Meow.

Nelson's voice stopped Martha in midmotion.

"Nelson," she said. "What do you want?"

Meow, Nelson mewed sweetly.

"Yes. Dogs can pick up a lot with their mouths. So what?"

Meow, meow.

"Prove it? No problem."

Martha picked up a rock with her mouth.

"Phwee?" She spit it out. "I mean, *see*? No problem."

Nelson's yellow eyes twinkled. *Meow?*

"You?" Martha said. "Of course, I could pick you up. Easy."

And that's just what she did.

A CRUMBY SURPRISE

As soon as Martha tried to lift Nelson gently with her teeth, he let out a loud, exaggerated *YOWL!*

Martha quickly dropped him. Nelson was no fun. Martha left him to go inside for a nap, but it wasn't two seconds before all the children gathered around her. Alice's older brother, Ronald, was holding Nelson. *Meow,* Nelson whimpered, looking wounded, as though he were about to faint.

"You shouldn't bite Nelson, Martha," said Helen.

"I didn't. I'm innocent!" Martha said.

Ronald cradled the limp cat in his arms.

"Poor kitty," Ronald cooed. "Look, there's slobber in his fur."

"Well, *you* try putting a cat in *your* mouth and see if you don't get . . ." Martha's voice trailed off. "This doesn't sound good, does it?"

Ronald scowled, and everyone looked at Martha.

"You're all biased!" Martha said. "You assume I'm guilty without hearing my side of the story."

"Martha," Helen said. "I'm sure you weren't trying to hurt Nelson, but Ronald would feel better if you stayed in the garage."

"I've been framed!" Martha cried. "I've been falsely accused. The cat set me up."

Helen walked Martha to the garage. "Look," Helen said, opening the door. "You've had a lot of biscuits. Why don't you take a nap here?"

"All right," Martha snapped. She lay on the garage floor. "I'll nap. But I won't like it! This is totally . . . "

Before she could finish, Martha was fast asleep. *Zzzzz.*

Back at the party, Alice announced, "Piñata time!"

"An electronic piñata?" T.D. said.

"My dad says it's the latest thing," Alice said. "There's only one problem."

She tapped the piñata with a stick. "YOU WIN!" it said. Pictures of candy danced across the screen.

"The candy's electronic, too," said Alice sadly.

Their game was interrupted by a shout from the kitchen.

"OH, NO!" Mrs. Boxwood exclaimed.

The kids ran inside.

"What's the matter, Mom?" Alice asked.

Standing by the table, Mrs. Boxwood held up Alice's birthday cake.

"Someone ate part of your cake!" Mrs. Boxwood said. "Who could have done this?"

"At least *I* didn't do it this time," said Alice, with relief.

Rx

Truman examined the cake. "It's not sliced, and there are no finger marks. It looks like an animal ate it."

"Animal?" Ronald said. "Hmm. I know what happened."

He marched to the garage. The other kids followed.

"Aha!" said Ronald, opening the garage door. "Look what's in front of Martha!"

Martha woke up, yawning. She looked at the floor. "Oh, hey! Are those cake crumbs? Yum!"

She licked them up.

"Admit it," said Ronald. "You're guilty. You ate my sister's cake!"

Martha raised her head. "CAKE! Where?"

"Don't act innocent," Ronald said.

"She *is* innocent," said Helen. "She wasn't anywhere near it."

"There's only one way to find out the truth," said Ronald. "Put Martha on trial! In a trial, you *have* to tell the truth."

He looked through some tools and found a mallet. "This will be my gavel. I'll be the judge."

"Oh no, you won't," Alice said, grabbing the gavel. "We need someone who's not biased to be the judge."

"Biased? *Me?*" Ronald said.

"Yes, *you,*" said Alice. "You've already made up your mind that Martha did it."

Alice handed the gavel to Truman. "Truman, you be the judge. The rest of us will be the jury. We'll decide if Martha is guilty or innocent."

"Jury duty?" said Carolina. "Yuck! I came for a party."

"Really? I came for cake," said Martha.

MARTHA INTERRUPTS

Excuse me. I have to interrupt the story. We're about to get to the part where I wasn't allowed to talk much. I'd like to make up for it now.

We all sat in the backyard for the trial. I'll sit for lots of things. Cake, for example. Instead I was sitting next to Truman, the judge, who kept telling me to be quiet.

In front of us, the jury—Alice, Carolina, and Helen—sat on two picnic benches.

"Order in the court!" Truman shouted. *BANG, BANG!* He slammed his gavel on the picnic table.

"No cake *and* no talking?" I said. "This isn't a party. This is a cruel joke!"

"Shhh," said Truman. "Ronald, present your evidence."

Ronald paced in front of the jury.

"First, we all know that cats are better than dogs," he said. "Dogs have fleas. Dogs stink."

What was Ronald talking about? I smell *great*.

"I object!" I said. "I don't stink! I smell different every day. It all depends on what I've rolled in. Today I smell like old shoes and banana peels. Fragrant and delightful!"

"Quiet, Martha!" Truman shouted. Then he said, "Ronald, that's not evidence."

"Well, it's what's wrong with dogs," Ronald said.

"Evidence isn't your opinion. Evidence is something that would help prove Martha is guilty of the crime," said Truman.

"Evidence?" Ronald repeated. "Like the cake crumbs?"

"Precisely."

"There were cake crumbs around Martha," Ronald said. "That proves she ate the cake. It's an open and shut case."

T.D. leaped to his feet. "Open and shut is right! The garage door was shut. How could a dog open it?"

"That's right. No hands!" I added.

"Then there's the crumbs," said T.D. "You like crumbs, don't you, Martha?"

"I do," I said. "I call them floor food."

"Why would Martha leave all those crumbs?" T.D. asked the court. "Answer? She wouldn't! Someone wanted Martha to look guilty. Someone had it in for Martha from the beginning. Someone like . . . NELSON!"

Nelson sat on the ground in front of the jury, looking fluffy and harmless. Drat him.

"Nelson?" Ronald said. "How could he do it? Look at him. He's so cute."

"*Que lindo,*" Carolina cooed, agreeing with Ronald.

Cute? I thought. Was I the only one who saw through his act?

"Hang on, T.D.," said Ronald. "You said a dog couldn't open a door. How could a cat?"

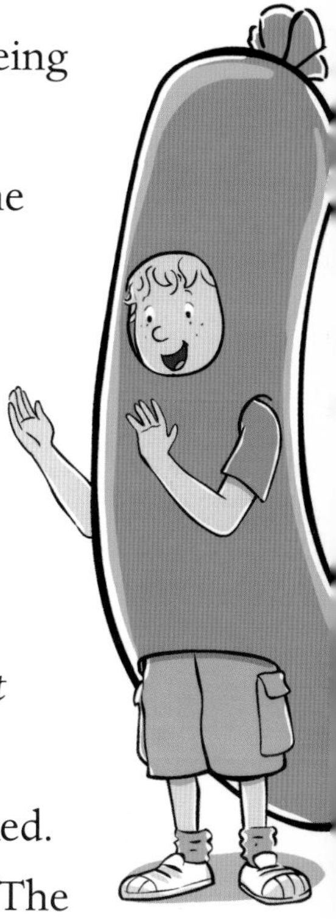

I wondered what T.D. could say now. He paused for a moment, and then he said, "Maybe the door *wasn't* opened!"

"What do you mean?" Ronald asked.

"The cat ate the cake," said T.D. "The problem was finding someone to take the blame. Here's how it went . . ."

Trust me: you won't believe how it went! I'll let you get back to the story to find out.

THE VERDICT

"Nelson is not your ordinary cat," T.D. said to the jury. "His skills will surprise you. After he ate the cake, he knew just what to do.

"He connected a wire to the ceiling and climbed up it. Then he took out his drill and opened an air duct. He crawled inside. Once Nelson was above the garage, he grabbed his blowtorch—"

"Nelson has a *blowtorch?*" Alice asked.

"Just let me tell the story," T.D. said. "He cut a hole in the garage ceiling.

"Then he slipped through the hole and quietly landed next to Martha. He wiped his whiskers and the cake crumbs fell to the floor."

"But how did he escape?" Helen asked.

"Through the window," T.D. said. "Nelson ran a wire from the garage window to a tree. He zipped across it.

"So you see," T.D. continued, "the garage door never had to be opened at all."

Ronald shook his head. "That's the most ridiculous thing I've ever heard. Martha is guilty. She ate the cake!"

Suddenly there was a pitiful sound from Nelson. *Meow-OW.*

"What's wrong with Nelson?" Martha asked.

Nelson looked queasy.

"Nelson!" Ronald cried. He watched his cat gag, and then . . .

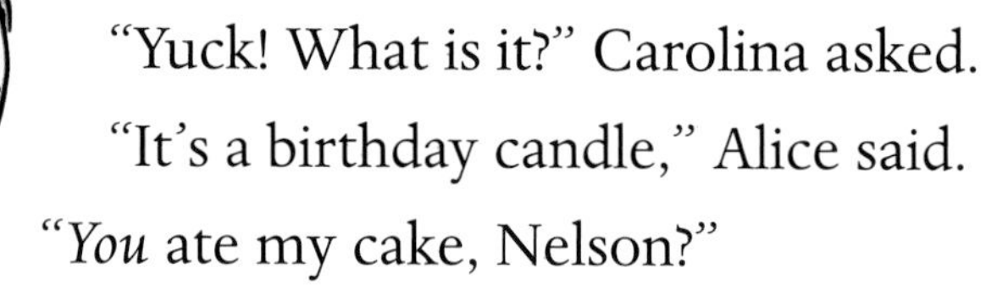

"Yuck! What is it?" Carolina asked.

"It's a birthday candle," Alice said. "*You* ate my cake, Nelson?"

Nelson wobbled. He swayed. He fell on his face.

"My poor baby!" Ronald said, scooping him up.

"You should take him to the vet," Martha suggested. "Maybe he ate more candles."

"Good thinking," said Alice.

Just then, Mrs. Boxwood walked into the yard. "I have another cake!" she sang, placing a box on the picnic table.

"Mom, we have to bring Nelson to the vet," Ronald said. "I'll explain on the way."

"Oh dear," said Mrs. Boxwood. She shook her head as she followed Ronald to the car. "Alice's parties are always an adventure."

As they left, the rest of the party eyed the cake.

"Cake!" Martha said. "Look at my tail go! I call this my cake dance."

"Order!" said Truman. "You're still on trial. Has the jury reached a verdict?"

"Not guilty!" the jury cheered.

"You're acquitted, Martha. You're exonerated of all charges," Truman said.

"Are you speaking English?" Martha asked.

"I mean, you're innocent," said Truman.

"In that case," said Alice, raising the gavel into the air. "I declare this trial . . . closed!"

She slammed the gavel down.

"NOOOO!" Helen and T.D. screamed at the same time.

"Hooray!" said Martha, licking frosting from her face. "What a party!"

MARTHA SPEAKS AGAIN

Thanks to Nelson, my first party wasn't *purr*fect. But even though I was put on trial, I still had fun. (Oh, and don't worry about Nelson. He's feeling better.)

Helen and I never did figure out how the crumbs got in the garage. But as we left Alice's, I noticed something.

A wire ran from her garage window to a tree. It might have been a clothesline. Or . . . is Nelson really an expert thief?

Nah!

Oh, well. I guess it'll just have to remain a mystery.

Keep reading for another mystery. See how I help crack this case!

Part Two

NO DOGS ALLOWED

I'm a pretty happy dog, Martha thought. But I'd be happier without three things: leashes, baths, and NO DOGS ALLOWED signs.

Martha stared at the Squiggy Piggy Mart's door. It had a picture of a dog with a slash through it.

"It's just rude," Martha said.

"You know dogs aren't allowed inside. It's the rules," said Helen. She tied Martha's leash to a parking meter. "I'll be right back."

Helen patted Martha's head and walked into the store.

"We should move to France!" Martha shouted. "French dogs get to go everywhere! They live like kings! Kings, I tell you!"

Hmph, Martha thought. *This is unfair. I'm not happy. Nothing could make me happy. Nothing! Not even—*

Martha smiled. "Hey, is that a cookie?"

In a stroller next to her, a baby held a mushy cookie.

"Bow-wow," said the baby.

"Yes," said Martha. "Doggies say 'bow-wow.' "

The baby pointed a crumb-covered finger at Martha.

"Let me clean you up," Martha said. She licked cookie crumbs off the baby's hand.

"Ahem," said the baby's mother.

Martha looked up. "Oh, hi! That's one smart baby you've got there. Tasty, too!"

The mother quickly pushed the stroller away.

"Bye, baby!" Martha called after them.

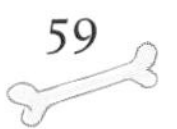

A car pulled up behind her, and two men stepped out. One was tall. The other was short. They both looked pretty scruffy.

Wow, Martha thought. *Those men look like they hate baths as much as I do.*

"Out of my way, mutt," said the tall one. He put coins into the meter.

"This job is going to be a piece of cake," said the short one.

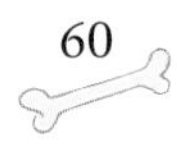

Cake? Mmm, Martha thought.

"It'll be like taking candy from a baby," said the other.

"Ahh, candy," said Martha. "Wait! Take? Baby? Oh, no! That poor baby!"

The men headed in the same direction as the stroller.

"Don't worry, baby!" Martha hollered. "No one's going to take your candy while I'm around!"

Martha ran after the men, but the leash stopped her short.

PLUMBING FOR FLOWERS

Helen walked out of the Squiggy Piggy Mart with a bag of groceries.

"Helen!" Martha cried. "Quick, untie me!"

Helen untied Martha's leash from the meter. "What's the rush?"

"We've got to stop a crime!" Martha said, taking off.

"WHOA!" Helen shouted. "*I'm* supposed to be walking *you!* What's going on?"

"I overheard two men discussing a plot," Martha said. "They mentioned candy . . . and babies . . . and cake! We have to act fast."

"But—" Helen said.

Martha stopped at the store the men had entered. She peered inside.

"I don't see anyone. We're too late!" she wailed. "Those men stole all the cake and probably that poor baby's candy, too!"

Then Martha spotted the men in a corner of the store. They spotted her, too.

"Duck!" said Martha.

"Martha!" said Helen. "Nobody robbed this store. It closed last month. Remember?"

The store door swung open. Martha gulped.

"Are you looking for something, kid?" the tall man asked.

"No," said Helen, blushing. "My silly dog thought the store was being robbed. But you must be opening a new store. What kind?"

"Plumbing," said one.

"Flowers," said the other at the same time.

The men glared at each other.

"Plumbing flowers?" Helen asked.

"It's a flower shop that sells plumbing stuff," the tall man mumbled. "It's easier to keep your flowers watered that way. Now beat it, kid."

The two men went back into the shop and slammed the door.

"Geesh. He'll need to work on his customer service skills," Helen said. "Let's go."

"But I'm positive those guys are criminals,"

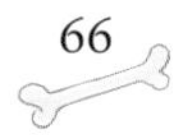

said Martha. "They're *very* suspicious. I don't trust them. Plus, they said they were going to take candy from a baby!"

"They weren't talking about a real baby," said Helen. "That's a figure of speech. You know, an expression? It's a funny way of saying something."

"Huh?" Martha said.

"If you say something will be like taking candy from a baby, you mean it'll be easy."

Martha was not convinced. "Plumbing-flower shop?" she said. "Doesn't that seem suspicious?"

Helen shrugged. "It's possible."

"It's also possible they're plotting a crime." Martha walked in circles, and as she walked, her leash wound around Helen's legs. "We have to trip them up!" she said, and took off running.

But the only one who tripped was Helen.

"Whoops," said Martha. "Sorry."

Can you believe that Helen didn't think those men were up to no good? It was obvious to me, but who listens to the dog?

Helen's friend T.D. came over for a game, and because we were playing catch, another member of the family joined us. Skits can't talk, but he's never met a flying object he didn't want to catch.

T.D. threw a flying disk and Skits leaped up and caught it in midair. He almost landed on me.

"Hey! Watch where you're going!" I said.

Woof, Skits barked.

"What nerve! Of course I could have caught it," I said. Sometimes I have to remind Skits that *I'm* the alpha dog. "I'm busy thinking. I'm trying to uncover a plot."

Woof, woof. Skits pawed at the ground.

"No," I explained. "Not a plot of land. A 'plot' like a plan. I think the guys I saw are plotting to commit a crime."

"Believe me," Helen said. "The only thing those guys are plotting is how to open a plumbing-flower shop."

But T.D. said, "I think Martha might be right. Something smells fishy."

"It's probably me," I said. "I rolled in something earlier. You like it? I thought it was frog, but maybe it was fish."

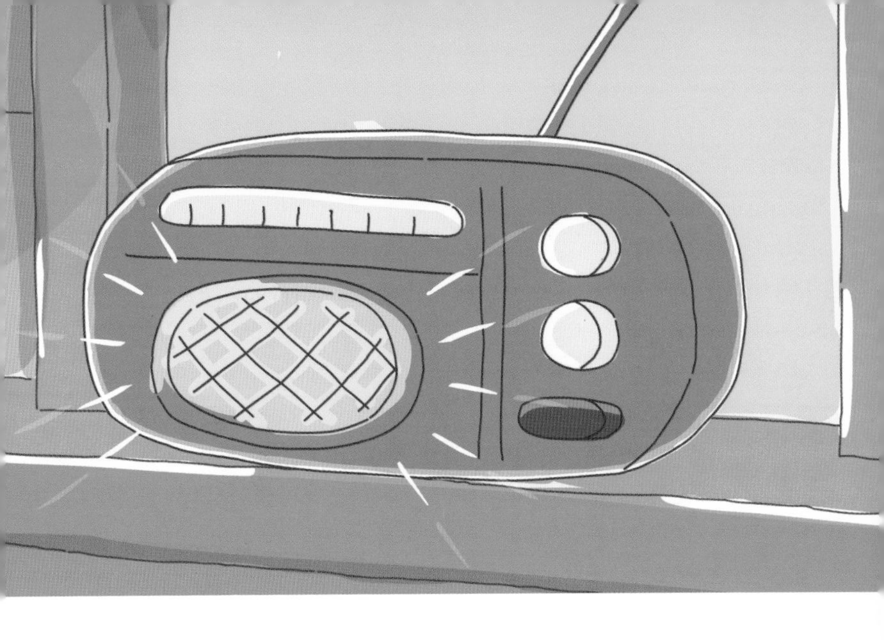

"It's an expression," said T.D. "If you say something smells fishy, you think it's suspicious. Those guys might be plotting to rob a bank or—"

T.D. was interrupted by news on the radio.

"This just in!" the DJ announced. "Police are on the lookout for safecracker Louie Kablooie and his accomplice, Jimmy Gimme. The criminals are believed to be in the area, plotting a robbery."

"Could it be the men we saw?" Helen said.

"It *has* to be," I said. "I knew I was right!" People are so slow to pick up what a dog knows right away.

"I need to see those men for myself," said T.D.

And before you could say "plumbing flowers," Helen, T.D., and I were next to the empty store. We watched the men talk inside. The tall one pointed to something on a map. The other nodded.

"Those two are Kablooie and Gimme," I whispered. "I'm positive. Look! They're probably pointing at the jewelry store on that map. That must be what they plan to rob!"

"Then why are they in an empty store across the street from it?" Helen asked.

“I know!” said T.D. “I saw it in a movie.” He took out his drawing pad. “They’re going to go into the empty store’s basement. They’ll dig a tunnel under the street and into the jewelry store’s basement. Then they’ll crack the safe and steal the jewels. It’s easy pickings.”

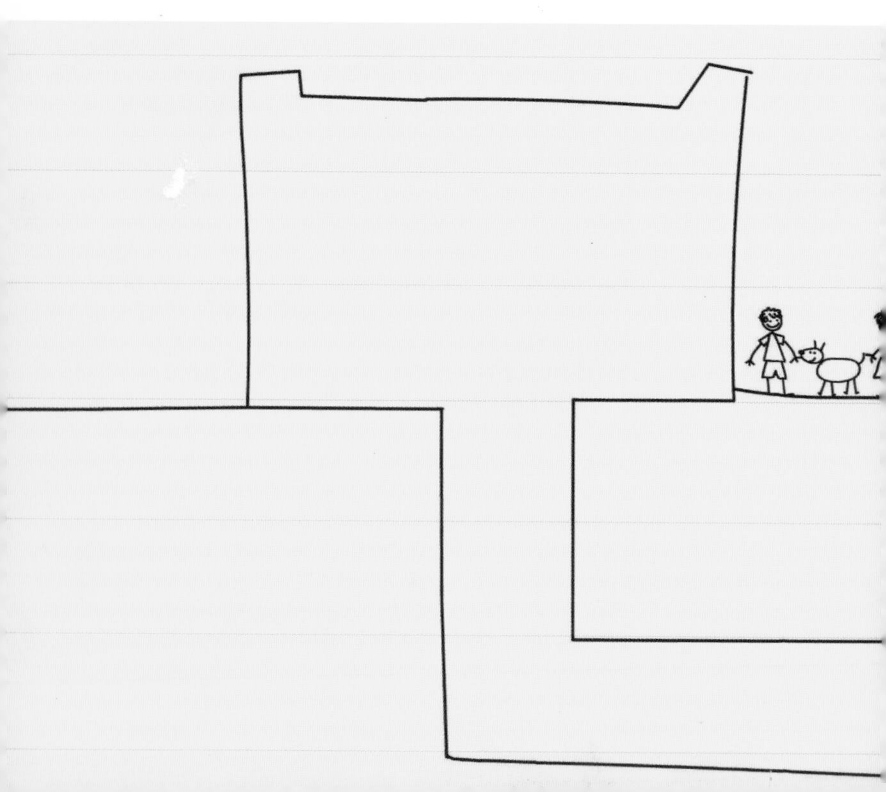

"Pickings?" I said. "There are fruit trees in the basement?"

Helen and T.D. threw up their arms. "It's an expression!" they shouted.

"People have too many expressions!" I said. "Well, how do we stop them?"

"Simple," said T.D. "I'll sneak inside and

redraw their map. Instead of digging into the jewelry store, they'll dig into the public pool. When they hit water, they'll slosh back into the tunnel. Then—POP!—they'll burst out of a manhole. We'll be waiting there with the cops!"

"One problem," Helen said. "The pool is two blocks away. They'd have to dig for weeks."

T.D. said, "I'm willing to wait."

"Maybe we should tell the police," Helen said.

"Then we'll need proof," I said. "You know, evidence? Something to convince the police that those guys are crooks."

Helen jumped to her feet. "I have an idea!"

And boy, did she!

SNOOPS

Back at Helen's house, Martha and T.D. watched Helen search for something in her bedroom.

"I know it's here somewhere," Helen said. "Martha and I just used it to make our own music video."

Finally, she found what she wanted.

"Ta-da!" said Helen, holding up a toy. "We'll catch the thieves with this! It's my Sing-and-Go karaoke machine."

"What are you going to do?" T.D. asked. "Sing until they surrender?"

Helen gave T.D. a hard look. "This has a built-in video camera. If those guys do anything suspicious, we'll record it. We'll show the tape to the police as proof that they're criminals."

"Good idea!" said T.D.

"Are you sure you want to be my accomplices?" Helen asked.

"Isn't an accomplice a person who helps somebody do something wrong?" Martha asked.

"Well, snooping *is* wrong," said Helen.

"But we're snooping to stop a crime," T.D. said. "We're more like *partners* than accomplices."

Helen smiled. "Okay then—partners?"

"Partners!" they said together.

Soon Martha, Helen, and T.D. were spying on the men once again. This time, they hid behind a mailbox next to the empty store.

Helen videotaped the suspects. She filmed them looking at a map. She filmed them watching the jewelry store.

"Are we missing anything?" asked Helen.

Martha's head popped in front of the lens.

"ME!" she said, posing. "Be sure to get my good side."

"Martha!" Helen and T.D. groaned.

Helen looked back at the store. "Uh-oh! They're leaving. Quick, hide!"

Crouched behind the mailbox, they

watched the men get into their car. The car sped off with a screech!

"That's all the proof we'll get," Martha said. "Let's take it to the police."

The police station was only a short walk away. Martha, Helen, and T.D. went straight to the chief.

"Louie Kablooie, eh?" the police chief said.

"This isn't like when you thought robots had taken over the toy store, is it?"

"No, sir," said T.D. "But in my defense, those robot costumes were really good."

"We have proof," said Helen, holding up the karaoke machine. "Take a look. It's Kablooie and his accomplice, all right."

Helen pressed play.

But instead of Louie Kablooie and Jimmy Gimme, Martha and Helen popped onto the screen. "OH, WHERE, OH, WHERE HAS MY LITTLE DOG GONE?" they sang. "OH, WHERE, OH—"

"NO! That's not it!" Helen said, covering her eyes.

"I've seen enough," said the police chief.

"Wait! You'll miss my big finish," Martha said.

On the screen, Martha rapped. "OH, WHERE CAN SHE BUH-BUH-BUH-*BE!*"

Helen grabbed the Sing-and-Go. "I must have hit the wrong track. The criminals are on here somewhere."

"Sure," said the chief, walking them to the door. "Don't worry. I'll check it out."

Outside the station, Helen sighed. "I don't think he believed us."

"Sure, he did," said Martha. "And I think he loved my big finish!"

"Well, there's only one way to know for sure," said T.D. "Let's go back to the empty store. We'll see if the police chief arrests those men."

Helen and Martha nodded.

They all walked back to the store.

Inside, the men had returned to their earlier positions. The tall one was watching the jewelry store. The other was taking notes. Neither one of them heard the back door creak open.

"How's it going?" said a deep voice behind them.

"Aah!" the waiting men hollered. They spun around.

"Oh, it's just you," said the tall one. "All is quiet."

"Keep watching," said the police chief. "All evidence suggests that Kablooie is planning to rob that jewelry store today."

“He’d better hurry,” the short man said. “It’s three o’clock. An armored car is coming to pick up the jewels at four.”

“If Kablooie strikes, we’ll be ready for him,” the police chief said. “Oh, and try not to be so obvious. A couple kids spotted you. They think you’re Kablooie and Gimme!”

Hiding behind the mailbox, Martha, Helen, and T.D. watched the three men laugh as if they’d just heard the funniest joke.

"Why isn't the chief arresting them?" Martha said. "How much proof does he need?"

Helen shrugged. "It's in the hands of the police now. Let's go home."

T.D. and Helen walked away. But Martha stayed behind.

"I can't let those guys rob the jewelry store," she said. "I have to do something!"

As the clock ticked, the two men waited.

"Kablooie's going to walk right into our trap," the tall man said. "As long as things stay nice and quiet." But at that moment . . .

"LOUIE KABLOOIE, COME OUT WITH YOUR HANDS UP!" Martha shouted into the Sing-and-Go microphone. "I REPEAT: COME OUT WITH YOUR HANDS—"

Her paw accidentally hit a wrong button.

"OH, WHERE, OH, WHERE CAN SHE BUH-BUH-BUH-*BE!*" came out instead.

Martha fumbled with the machine. "Ugh, paws!"

"Yes, press *pause!*" said a voice.

Martha looked up. It was the short man. The tall one stood next to him. They looked even angrier than before.

"We need to talk," said the tall man.

"Bow-wow?" she said.

"Nice try, talking dog," said the short one. "I'm Officer O'Reilly. Minetti here is my partner. We're trying to catch thieves robbing that jewelry store."

He showed Martha two mug shots.

Uh-oh. The real Kablooie and Gimme look nothing like these cops, Martha thought.

"Gee, I'm sorry I was suspicious of you, officers," Martha said. "I feel awful."

"Just stay out of our way," Minetti said. "Kablooie should be here any minute. The last thing we need is some rapping mutt messing things up."

And with that, they walked away. As she stood alone on the sidewalk, Martha's ears drooped.

The men returned to the store. They checked the time.

Tick, TOCK! The clock struck four.

The men looked at the jewelry store.

"There's the armored car," said Minetti, looking through binoculars. "But where's Kablooie? I guess we were wrong about him."

"He must be hitting another jewelry store," O'Reilly said.

Minetti packed up his things. "Our work here is done."

Martha decided to go home. She picked up the karaoke machine in her mouth.

Not only did I blow the case, but I'm getting Helen's toy all slobbery, too, she thought.

Just then, the slam of a heavy metal door caught her attention. Martha looked up to see the armored truck. It was still in front of the jewelry store. A security guard had stepped out of it.

That guy looks familiar, she thought.

Martha's jaw dropped. The Sing-and-Go fell to the ground.

"Sizzling sausages!" she cried. "That's no security guard! It's Louie Kablooie!"

Martha raced to the empty store. She looked inside.

"Oh, no! The cops are gone!" she said. "What do I do?"

Martha thought fast. She needed help.

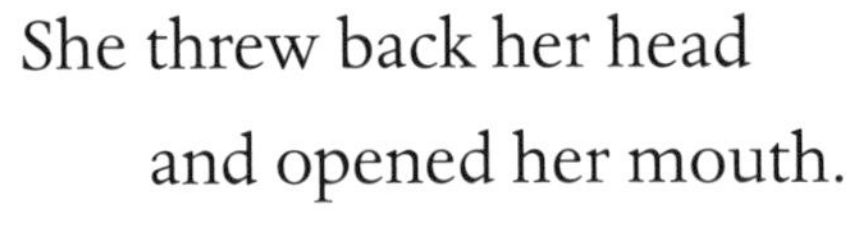

She threw back her head and opened her mouth.

Ahwooooo! Her howl traveled to every corner of Wagstaff City.

In a bathtub, a boxer raised his soapy head. On a porch step, a Dalmatian perked up his ears. All across town dogs heard Martha's howl. They streamed out their doors and into the streets. Soon they were one large pack running toward Martha's call for help.

My dog friends better hurry, Martha thought. *Kablooie and Gimme are already leaving the store with bags. They're about to make their getaway!*

"See?" Kablooie said. "Piece of cake."

"But boss, I didn't get any cake. I only got jewels," Gimme replied.

"It's an expression, you nitwit!" Kablooie said. "Let's get these bags into the truck!"

The sound of barking began to fill the air.

"What's all that racket?" Kablooie said, reaching for the truck's door.

WOOF! ARF! YIP! The barks grew louder.

A mob of dogs began to surround the truck.

"Yikes!" said Kablooie, dropping his bag. He raised his hands into the air.

"We're trapped!" said Gimme. He dropped his bag, too.

"Way to go, dogs!" Martha shouted. "Keep Kablooie and his accomplice in line. Grab their bags. We'll need them as evidence."

Two dogs dragged the bags away with their teeth.

Down the street, sirens blared. Red lights flashed. The police chief's car arrived at the scene.

"You two are going to jail for a long time," the chief said.

"That's just an expression, right?" said Gimme.

"Nope," said Martha. "You're really going to jail!"

"And it's all thanks to—" the police chief puffed up his chest and rapped, "MUH-MUH-MUH-*MARTHA!*"

Martha wagged her tail. "Now that's what I call a big finish!"

MARTHA SAYS GOODBYE

It was a proud moment for us dogs. The police chief thanked me. Even Officer O'Reilly and Officer Minetti seemed impressed.

That night, I watched the news with Helen.

"Tonight's top story," said the reporter. "Police caught

expert safecracker Louie Kablooie and his accomplice, Jimmy Gimme. The police were aided by a secret partner. They wouldn't reveal the identity, saying she's only known by her code name: Martha."

Helen didn't say a word. But she gave me an extra belly rub.

Now, one thing is for sure. The police station will never have a NO DOGS ALLOWED sign. And that makes me one happy dog!

ANK
JEWELR